My first web

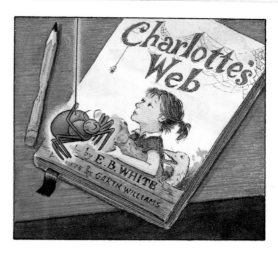

My favorite book, *Charlotte's Web*

Baby picture of me and Grampa

For the girls—
Meghan, Jacqueline, Theresa,
Kerry, and Amanda
—D.C.

For Valerie
—H.B.

Joanna Cotler Books is an imprint of HarperCollins Publishers.

Diary of a Spider   Text copyright © 2005 by Doreen Cronin   Illustrations copyright ©
2005 by Harry Bliss   Manufactured in China. All rights reserved. No part of this book
may be used or reproduced in any manner whatsoever without written permission except in
the case of brief quotations embodied in critical articles and reviews. For information address
HarperCollins Children's Books, a division of HarperCollins Publishers, 195 Broadway,
New York, NY 10007.   www.harpercollinschildrens.com

Library of Congress Cataloging-in-Publication Data   Cronin, Doreen.   Diary of a spider / by Doreen Cronin ; pictures
by Harry Bliss.—1st ed.   p. cm.   Summary: A young spider discovers, day by day,
that there is a lot to learn about being a spider, including how to spin webs and
avoid vacuum cleaners.   ISBN 978-0-06-000153-7 (trade bdg.) — ISBN 978-0-06-223300-4 (paper-
over-board)   ISBN 978-0-06-000154-4 (lib. bdg.)   [1. Spiders—Fiction. 2. Insects—Fiction. 3. Diaries—Fiction.]   I. Bliss, Harry, 1964- ill. II. Title.   PZ7.C88135Dg 2005
2004011549 [E]—dc22   2005
16 SCP 4   First Edition

Typography by Alicia Mikles

By Doreen Cronin • Pictures by Harry Bliss

DIARY OF A SPIDER

Joanna Cotler Books
An Imprint of HarperCollinsPublishers

Today was Grandparents Day at school, so I brought Grampa with me.

He taught us three things:

1. Spiders are not insects—insects have six legs.

2. Without spiders, insects could take over the world.

3. Butterflies taste better with a little barbecue sauce.

MARCH 16

Grampa says that in his day, flies and spiders did not get along.

MARCH 29

Today in gym class we learned how to catch the wind so we could travel to faraway places.

When I got home, I made up
flash cards so I could practice:

2.
Release
silk.

1.
Climb
high.

3.
Catch
wind.

Fly made up her own flash card:

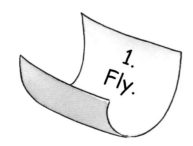

1.
Fly.

I'm starting to
see why Grampa
doesn't like her.

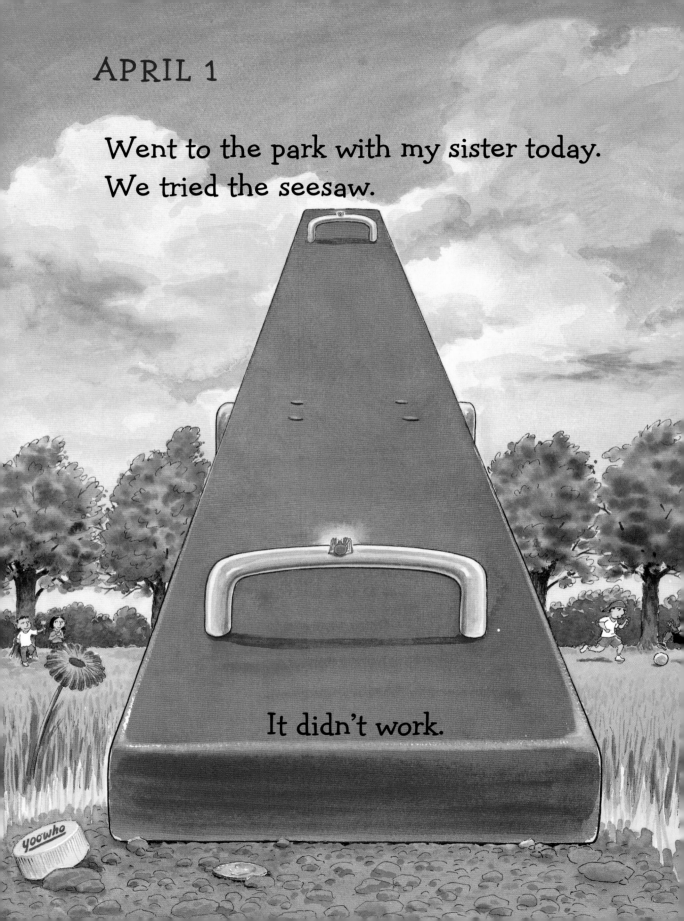

We tried the tire swing.

It didn't work.

We spun a huge sticky web
on the water fountain.

That worked.

EEEEEEK!

APRIL 12

Today was Safety Day at school. We learned that vacuums eat spiderwebs and are very, very dangerous. If we hear a vacuum, we should Stop, Drop, and Run.

STOP WHAT WE'RE DOING. DROP FROM THE WEB. RUN LIKE CRAZY.

PARTY CANDLES 40 CT.

CANDLES

APRIL 13

We had a vacuum drill today.
I stopped what I was doing.

Forgot where I was going.

And ran screaming from the room.

We're having another drill tomorrow.

I'm sleeping over at Worm's house tonight.

I hope they don't have leaves and rotten tomatoes for dinner again.

MAY 8

Today was show-and-tell.
So I brought in my old skin.

My teacher called on it to
lead the Pledge of Allegiance.

Daddy Longlegs made fun of Fly because she eats with her feet. Now she won't come out of her tree house.

I'm going to find him
and give him a piece
of my mind!

JUNE 6

I found Daddy
Longlegs.

He's a lot bigger
than I thought
he was.

I gave him a piece
of my lunch
instead.

JUNE 7

Fly's tree house blew away
in the wind today.

So did Grampa.

JUNE 18

I got a postcard from
Grampa today:

PARIS - FRANCE

Spider
5 Web Ave.
Arachnidville
05400
USA

Dear Spider,
Ooh-la-la!
I landed in Paris!
French bugs are
delicious!
Au revoir,
Grampa

leg
of
French
gnat...
→
give it a try!

Tanet co.

JUNE 30

Grampa came home today.

I couldn't wait to hear about
how he rode the winds
all the way over the ocean!

Turns out, he caught a breeze to the
airport and napped in first class.

JULY 9

Today was my birthday.
Grampa decided I was
old enough to
know the secret
to a long, happy life:

Never fall asleep in a shoe.

JULY 16

Things I scare:

1. Fly's mom

2. Tiny bugs

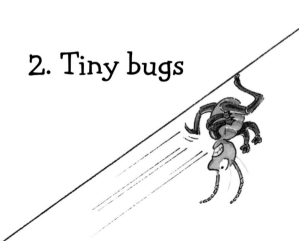

3. People using water fountains at the park

Things that scare me:

1. Daddy Longlegs

2. Vacuums

3. People with big feet

I wish that people wouldn't judge all spiders based on the few spiders that bite.

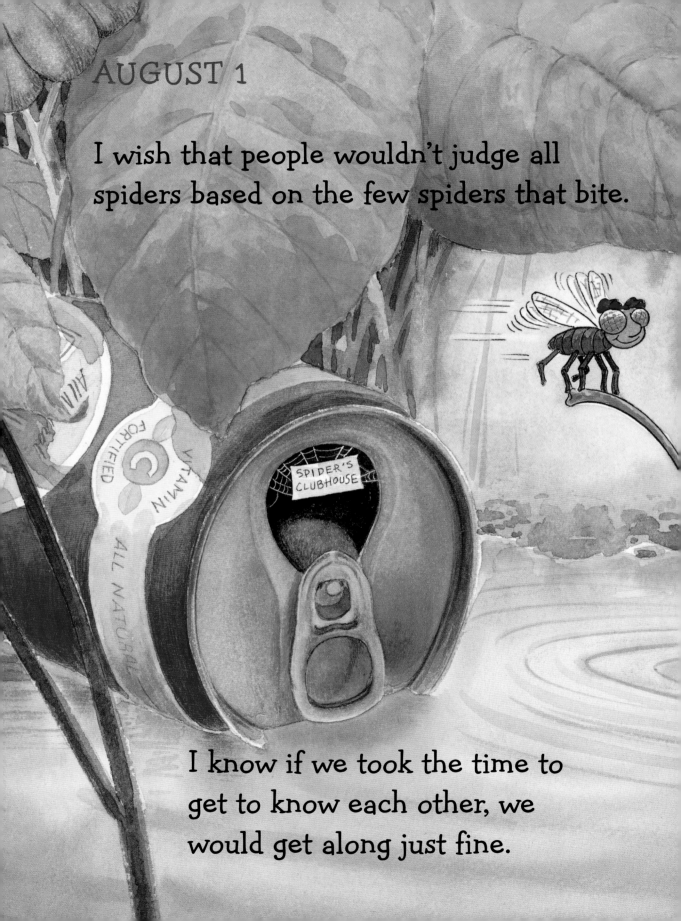

I know if we took the time to get to know each other, we would get along just fine.

Just like me and Fly.

Dad made me this!

Worm found this!